Oh, My! Ginny Fry!

The Halloween Mix-Up

by Gina Shaw
Illustrated by Patrice Barton

Scholastic Inc.
New York Toronto London Auckland
Sydney Mexico City New Delhi Hong Kong

To Micah—May you grow up
to love reading as much as
your mommy and daddy do.
—G.S.

To Matt, Colin, and Laura—P.B.

ISBN 978-0-545-24384-1

Text copyright © 2010 by Gina Shaw
Illustrations copyright © 2010 by Patrice Barton
All rights reserved. Published by Scholastic Inc.

SCHOLASTIC and associated logos are trademarks
and/or registered trademarks of Scholastic Inc.
Lexile is a registered trademark of MetaMetrics, Inc.

12 11 10 9 8 7 6 5 4 3 2   10 11 12 13 14 15/0

Printed in the U.S.A.   40
First printing, October 2010

Book design by Jennifer Rinaldi Windau

Chapter 1

"Good morning, Class 1-11!"

Ms. Hurley says.

"Good morning, Ms. Hurley!"

we all say back.

"Halloween is right around the

corner," she says. "Please look

at the calendar. Who can tell

me when it is?"

I raise my hand as high as I can.

I wave it in the air.

"Yes, Ginny," Ms. Hurley says. "Thank you for raising your hand today."

"Which corner?" I ask.

"What do you mean?" she asks.

I stare at Ms. Hurley.

"Which corner is Halloween around?"

Ms. Hurley smiles her teacher smile.

"That's just a saying," she says. "It

means that Halloween is almost here."

Then, Jody raises her hand.

Ms. Hurley calls on her.

"Tomorrow is Halloween," Jody says.

"That's right!" Ms. Hurley says. "Since

we are studying the food groups,

everyone will dress up as a food."

"Yayyy!" we shout.

Chapter 2

During math time, Ms. Hurley says, "Today we are going to learn about pairs. Who can tell me how many items make a pair?"

Spike raises his hand.

Spike is my best friend.

He is so smart.

He knows the answers to lots of

Ms. Hurley's questions.

Spike always raises his hand.

He never shouts out.

Ms. Hurley likes that.

"Yes, Spike," Ms. Hurley says.

"Two items make a pair,"

Spike says.

"Like a pair of sneakers," I shout out.

Uh-oh! Ms. Hurley does not like that.

"Ginny," she says, "no shouting out!"

"Sorry!" I say.

"Any other pairs?" Ms. Hurley asks.

Jody raises her hand and says,

"A pair of earrings."

Ms. Hurley calls on Dustin.

"A pair of mittens," he says.

9

"Good!" Ms. Hurley says. "Spike is right. A pair means *two* of the same thing. Now, let's practice counting by 2s."

"2, 4, 6, 8," everyone says together.

I love to count.

I love to sing.

I shout out, "Who do we appreciate?

Ms. Hurley! Ms. Hurley! Yayyy!"

Everyone in the class stops.

All the boys and girls look at me.

The room is very quiet.

So, I shout my chant again,

"2, 4, 6, 8, who do we appreciate?

Ms. Hurley! Ms. Hurley! Yayyy!"

But Ms. Hurley does not like

this chant.

I can tell by the look on her face.

"Ginny," she says, "how many times do I have to remind you? No shouting out. You need to take a time-out."

Uh-oh! Too bad for me!

Chapter 3

After my time-out, it's lunchtime.

I sit with Spike.

I always sit with Spike.

But today, Spike isn't talking.

"What are you thinking about?"

I ask him.

"My Halloween costume," he says.

"I don't know what food to be."

"I'm going to be a neon orange carrot," I say. "And you can be a skinny, green string bean or a scarlet red apple."

"Thanks for the ideas," Spike says. "But I want to be something that no one else will be."

"Yeah," I say. "I do, too!"

Yayyy for us!

Chapter 4

"Stop, look, and listen," Ms. Hurley

sings out after lunch.

"O-kay," we all sing back.

"This afternoon we're going to make

trick-or-treat bags," Ms. Hurley says.

"Bond will hand out the paper bags.

Take out your crayons."

I love to draw.

I love to color.

I love all of the crayons in my

Bright and Bold box.

I jump up and down.

I pour my crayons onto

my desk.

Most of them fall on the floor.

Ms. Hurley looks at me.

"Ginny, please sit down. Put your crayons back in their box. Only take out one color at a time," she says.

I do what Ms. Hurley says.

I have so much fun making my trick-or-treat bag.

I draw a jack-o'-lantern and color it
in with my pumpkin orange crayon.
Spike draws a shiny, silver ghost
on his bag.
Then, he adds a creepy, jet-black
spider hanging from a long thread.
His bag is scary.

My bag is funny.

My pumpkin has a crooked smile
and three large, white teeth.

Soon, Ms. Hurley tells us to put away
our crayons.

She collects our trick-or-treat bags.

"I will return them to you tomorrow
at our party," Ms. Hurley tells us. "Don't
forget to wear an orange shirt for our
Halloween skit. And, be sure to bring
your costumes for our parade."

Yayyy for us!

Chapter 5

Friday is October 31.

It is Halloween.

Everyone is excited.

I walk over to Spike's desk.

"What's your costume?" I ask.

"You'll see," Spike says. "I want

to surprise you. What's your

costume?"

"I'm not telling if you're not
telling," I say. "I want to surprise
you, too."

I walk back to my desk and sit down.

"Good morning, boys and girls,"
Ms. Hurley says. "Happy Halloween!"

"Happy Halloween!" we all say back.

"I see everyone has an orange shirt on today," Ms. Hurley adds. "Let's line up to go to the auditorium."

We walk quietly in the hallway.

We find our seats.

We watch all of the other classes
put on their Halloween skits.
Then, it is our turn.
We all go onstage and face the
audience.
We watch Ms. Hurley.
She gives us the signal to start
singing.

Five little pumpkins sit on a gate.

The first one says, "It's getting late!"

The second one says, "There
are witches in the air!"

The third one says, "But we
don't care."

The fourth one says, "Let's
run and run."
The fifth one says, "We're ready
for some fun."
OOOOOO-OOOO goes the wind and
OUT goes the light, and the five
little pumpkins roll out of sight.

28

When we're done, the audience

claps and claps.

We take a bow.

Some teachers snap pictures.

We all smile.

Then, we walk off the stage

and line up.

"That was wonderful, Class 1-11!"

Ms. Hurley says. "I'm so proud of

all of you!"

Yayyy for us!

Chapter 6

We walk back to our classroom

and sit in our seats.

"Row 1, you may go to the closet and

get your costumes," Ms. Hurley says.

I'm in Row 1.

I go to the closet.

I look and look.

But I can't find my costume.

Ms. Hurley calls each row.

I'm still at the closet.

I'm still looking and looking.

Everyone starts to get dressed.

Where is my costume? I wonder.

I go back to my desk.

I take everything out of it.

No costume!

I open my backpack.

I take everything out of it.

No costume!

I look up.

I watch as everyone gets dressed.

I see a flash of yellowish green.

I look at Spike.

I race over to him.

"You have my costume!" I shout.

"Give it back to me."

"I do not!" Spike yells.

I pull at the costume.

Spike pulls back.

"RE-GI-NA! BRI-AN!" Ms. Hurley yells.

Those are our real names.

They are on our official school records.

Ms. Hurley uses them when she's

unhappy with us.

"What is going on?" Ms. Hurley asks.

"Why are you fighting?"

I start to speak very quickly.

"Spike-took-my-costume!" I explain.

"And-I-want-it-back. I-don't-want-him-to-wear-it!"

"This is my costume," Spike says.

"My stepdad helped me make it."

"My-mom-helped-me-make-mine," I say. "And-this-is-it! I-want-to-wear-my-costume."

"Slow down," Ms. Hurley says.

"Ginny, this is Spike's costume. It came from his backpack. But I think I know what happened."

Ms. Hurley walks to her desk.

I follow her.

She picks up a pile of clothing.

"I found this outside of our room this morning," Ms. Hurley says.

"You must have dropped it."

Oh, no!

"Sorry, Spike," I say. "Sorry, Ms. Hurley."

I feel bad.

I slink back to my desk and put on

my costume.

Now, Spike comes running over to me.

He is shouting.

"You stole my idea!" he yells.

"No, I didn't," I shout louder. "I didn't

even know what your idea was!"

Then, we look at each other.

Spike and I have the same costume!

Too bad for us!

Chapter 7

Ms. Hurley comes over to us again.

"What are you shouting about now?"
she asks.

"We have the same costume!" we
both say at the same time.

"And I wanted to have a costume
that no one else has," adds Spike.

Ms. Hurley looks at us.

All of the kids in the class look
at us.

We look at each other.

Then, we start to laugh.

I run to my desk.

I take out two pieces of paper.

I write some words on them.

I use my grass green crayon.

I tape one piece of paper to
Spike's costume.

I tape the other piece to my
costume.

We stand side by side.

I take Spike's hand.

Jody reads what I wrote
out loud.

"A pair of pears!" she says.

Everyone laughs.

Then, everyone claps.

Ms. Hurley smiles her

teacher smile.

We all line up for the parade.

Dustin is an apple.

Jody is a box of cereal.

Bond is a pea pod.

There is a strawberry,

a glass of milk,

a tomato, a potato,

and even a meatball.

There are lots of foods.

But there is only one pair of

pears!

We go outside to the playground.

All of the other classes in the school

are there, too.

We walk around in a large circle.

We all show off our costumes.

After the parade, we go back

to our room.

Ms. Hurley gives us our

trick-or-treat bags.

They are filled with treats.

Ms. Hurley reads us a

Halloween story.

Spike sits next to me.

We smile at each other.

What a great Halloween!

Yayyy for us!